12137587

GW00726958

AN UNOFFICIAL MINECRAFT BOOK
DIARY OF A
MINECRAFT
WOLF

SURREY LIBRARIES	
12137587	
Askews & Holts	09-Jan-2024
JF	

First published by Scholastic in Australia, 2023
This edition published by Scholastic in the UK, 2024
1 London Bridge, London, SE1 9BG
Scholastic Ireland, 89E Lagan Road, Dublin Industrial Estate,
Glasnevin, Dublin, D11 HP5F

SCHOLASTIC and associated logos are trademarks and/or
registered trademarks of Scholastic Inc.

Text copyright © Scholastic Australia, 2023.
Illustrations copyright © Scholastic Australia, 2023.
Cover and internal design by Hannah Janzen.
Typeset by Laura Ye.

ISBN: 978 0702 33313 2

A CIP catalogue record for this book is available from the British Library.

All rights reserved.
This book is sold subject to the condition that it shall not, by way of trade or
otherwise, be lent, hired out or otherwise circulated in any form of binding or cover
other than that in which it is published. No part of this publication may be
reproduced, stored in a retrieval system, or transmitted in any form or by any other
means (electronic, mechanical, photocopying, recording or otherwise) without
prior written permission of Scholastic Limited.

Printed and bound in Great Britain by Clays Ltd, Elcograf S.p.A
Paper made from wood grown in sustainable forests and other controlled sources.

1 3 5 7 9 10 8 6 4 2

www.scholastic.co.uk

MIX
Paper | Supporting
responsible forestry
FSC® C018072

AN UNOFFICIAL MINECRAFT BOOK

DIARY OF A MINECRAFT WOLF

PLAYER ATTACK

SCHOLASTIC

Oof!

Smash!

COMMANDO ROLL!

Jump! Perfect landing!

OH NO! TAKING FIRE!
PEW PEW PEW!

Duck! Take cover! Laser scope.

Explosions! **BRACE FOR IMPACT!**

Steady now ... Check for bad guys ...

THERE!

Target acquired, I repeat, target acquired. Teeth armed and ready.

"Winston?"

No time for distractions.

I licked my sharp wolf teeth and prepared to pounce on my prey. I stretched my claws in the dirt...

AND **LEAPED!**

My sharp jaws closed savagely on
my target and I shook my head,
tearing it into little pieces.

I WON!

"**Take that!**" I growled.

"Winston Wolf, where are you?"

I looked around and dropped my **prey** when I saw who was coming towards me.

"Right here, High Commander Wolf!"

A tan-coloured wolf approached me and I stood to attention. All GUARDs knew to be respectful of their leaders.

"Great to see you practising your striking skills," she said, "but when

we're at home, you can just call
me **Mum**."

I relaxed and grinned at her. When
you live in a Minecraft wolf pack,
it's pretty cool to have a High
Commander for a mum. She leads
the **HOWL COUNCIL – THE
HIGH ORDER OF WOLF
LEADERSHIP** – alongside High
Commanders Okami and Rolfe. Not
only does she run things around here,
but she knows nearly **everything**
and tells **everyone** what to do.

Sort of like what mums normally do
at home, except on a bigger scale.

"You know GUARDs don't really do all that **action hero stuff,** don't you?" she asked. "Our job is about security and protection. I don't want you to get your hopes up expecting a lot of excitement." She paused, frowning. "Winston, are those my towels?"

"What? Oh. Yeah."

All the towels she had hung on the washing line were now lying on the ground, chewed and ripped to shreds. What can I say? I'm a **canine,** after all. Some things can't be helped.

"I was using them for target practice," I explained as I helped her clean up. "GUARD training starts tomorrow and I want my skills to be **sharp**."

All **GUARDS – GUARDIANS UNITED AGAINST REAL DANGERS,** though regular mobs just call us Minecraft wolves – have to pass a training assessment before they can be sent on official assignments. I was really looking forward to mine – **I wasn't nervous at all! Not one bit.**

Well, maybe *one* bit. But that's it.

"How odd," Mum said. "I'm sure Okami said training for new recruits started today."

"No, Mum," I laughed. She was so forgetful! "He said it starts on Monday."

"Winston, today *is* Monday."

WHAT?!

I dropped the towels, yelled goodbye to my mum — who wasn't so forgetful after all — and **BOLTED** out of our little cave. I couldn't believe I'd forgotten what day it was! Mum had it on the calendar and everything — she knew it was important to me.

Our cave was part of a huge network of tunnels called **THE DEN.** As I leaped through the tunnels, my **wolf eyes** saw easily in the darkness. I needed to get to the training area in the very centre, deep underground, as fast as my paws could take me.

That's where today's training was. I didn't want to be late — not if I wanted to become a **REAL GUARD WOLF.**

I rounded a corner and the training ground's obstacle course came into view. Some other young wolves about my own age stood waiting with an older black wolf I knew well. I could tell from his expression that he was not happy.

"I'M SORRY!" I shouted, running down the slope towards the obstacle course. I was so close, but then one of my toes caught on a loose rock on the cavern floor. I **flipped** and landed flat on my snout, then skidded the rest of the way down the dirt slope. **Does no-one clean up around here?!**

I stopped right at the polished paws of High Commander Okami. The loose rock rolled to a stop beside me.

"We should probably have less rocks lying around," I said as I got up. "It's a **trip hazard.**"

"It's an underground cave, Winston."
Okami didn't look impressed, but he
didn't comment on my dirty face,
or the fact that I was late. **OOPS**.
He turned to face the whole group.
"Now that we're all here, it's time to
begin your training."

I shook with excitement. I had been
looking forward to this moment my
whole life — my chance to become
a real GUARD, just like my mum!
**NOTHING COULD POSSIBLY
GO WRONG NOW!**

Okay, so **a couple of things** went wrong. But just little things.

Like, I fell off some of the equipment on the obstacle course. Just the vertical rock wall. And the balance beam. And high ropes.

Oh yeah, and I **FACE-PLANTED** doing army crawls. But only because I hadn't realized Felicia Fang was going to be in my class!

Felicia's the fiercest wolf in our entire pack, with the quickest bite of any wolf I know. **She's incredible.** I looked over at her a few times and I swear she was looking right at me. It was amazing.

Unfortunately, that was when I fell down. Because I was distracted. I'm usually very good at obstacles. **I'm basically an athlete.**

Also, I made a **tiny boo-boo** in the teamwork challenge.

"Alright, everyone," Okami had said. "First team to capture the flag, wins."

I was teamed up with Lobo when we got into groups. Lobo is the same age as me, but bigger and **really bossy.** He briefed my team on our strategy and I was totally listening, but I was also biting my claws at the same time to keep them sharp.

A whistle blew and suddenly the game was **AFOOT!** Ha ha ... see what I did there?

The recruits began running in different directions, and I saw Felicia Fang looking around under a tree.

"What are you looking for?" I asked, hoping to be helpful.

"Just that flag. Have you seen it?"

OH THAT'S RIGHT! We were looking for a flag as a team. I helped her climb the tree so she could get a better view.

"I CAN SEE IT!" she exclaimed, and we raced off to snatch it up.

"WE DID IT!" I boasted, as Felicia captured the undefended flag. She cheered.

"WINSTON!" Okami shouted. "You just helped the wrong team capture **YOUR TEAM'S FLAG!**"

Ohhhh ... OOPS!

My team was pretty mad.

After that was a boring task where I had to sit there and read some assignment reports that had ... that ...

"**WINSTON!**"

"Huh? Wha — ?"

"Is that drool on the assignment reports? Were you **asleep?**"

"I was ... strategizing," I improvised.
I couldn't remember what Okami
had asked me to do with the
reports — something boring,
I'm sure. "And I did read them,
I swear."

I even had several papers
scattered in front of me to prove it.

"Really?" Okami didn't look convinced.
"And what did all these reports
have in common?"

I sat up.

OH! Now I understood the task.

"Well," I started excitedly, "I noticed that on every occasion, Intelligence reported that **BABY TURTLES** were found somewhere nearby. Under rocks, in the water. Whether our teams were guarding precious minerals, patrolling villages or chasing away pesky players, whenever something went wrong, there was a baby turtle somewhere in the area. It's all very suspicious. Do you think they could be the **masterminds** of all trouble in the Overworld?"

Okami stared at me. I was definitely onto something here!

"Um … no, Winston. I do not think baby turtles are criminal masterminds." He frowned. "You didn't notice **anything else** the reports had in common?"

"Uhh …" I thought about it. "They're all written in English?"

Okami sighed. "These assignments all occurred in the ocean biome. That suggests a **crime hotspot** where our GUARDs are likely to be requested in the future. You didn't pick up on that?"

"Huh," I said, looking down at the

reports. "I guess that explains all the baby turtles. Maybe someone should launch an investigation?"

"GUARDs don't investigate," Okami sniffed. "We **guard**."

Later, during silence training, I kept asking the other kids what flavour ice cream they like best — I mean, it's a tie between rabbit flavour and llama with choc chips, right? But it turns out that you're not meant to talk during silence training. **HONEST MISTAKE.**

"Winston," Okami asked me while

everyone else was eating lunch. "Have you been practising any of these skills?"

"Yes, all my life!" I said cheerfully.

"I mean..." The High Commander hesitated. "Are you sure you want to be a GUARD?"

"OF COURSE! I want to be like my mum. Besides, all wolves grow up to become GUARDs."

Every wolf eventually finds their place as a GUARD, whether that's patrolling outside in the biomes, or operating as a **DOG – A DEN-ORIENTED GUARD** – specializing in Engineering, Research or Tech Support. And while the jobs inside the Den are important, there's nothing **cooler** than GUARDs sneaking around the Overworld in squadrons, looking like ordinary mobs, but actually carrying out **super important assignments** for the HOWL Council.

I was looking forward to having my own earpiece so I could whisper orders to the other GUARDs in my pack. I bet you didn't even know that's how wolves communicate.

"That's very noble of you, Winston, but have you considered that perhaps your ... *talents* ... might be **different** from the other recruits?"

I got out my sheep sandwich and nodded. **HE WAS SO RIGHT!** I was way more talented than those other pups!

"Yeah, I'm very **unique** for a wolf," I agreed. "My mum says I am curious and observant."

"Are you sure she didn't say nosy and distracted?"

"What?"

"Nothing. How do you think you'll go with combat training for the Strike Force tomorrow?"

I **grinned** with all my wolfish teeth. Maybe I wasn't cut out for the Security Squad — you know, the plain-clothed GUARDs who patrol biomes to keep mobs safe. And maybe I wasn't meant for Intelligence — the team of wolves who send GUARDs information and guide them on each assignment. **But I could definitely be a GUARD in the Strike Force!**

You saw those towels. They didn't stand a chance against me and my **SKILLS.**

Good thing too, because wolves in the Strike Force have the **most important** job of all. They're the ones trained in combat, ready to protect mobs from any sudden attacks. They're the ones who risk their lives and face the **TRUE ENEMIES.**

TUESDAY

"PLAYERS!"

High Commander Rolfe made the whole class **jump** in terror as he spiked a sharp claw through the **WANTED** poster of a player.

"You've all heard the stories," he said, now marching back and forth. "There is always something going wrong in the Overworld, and the culprit is almost always a **player**. Troublesome, meddlesome and just **PLAIN ANNOYING**. That's why you're here. Our pack needs protection, and this enemy needs to be **stopped**."

I kept my back straight and my chin high like the other recruits, but my back legs were shaking a little. I mean, even if you're super brave like I am, is there anything scarier than an enemy you've never faced?

"This is why we train our GUARDs so hard," Mum said. She and the other High Commanders were here to coach our combat lesson. "GUARD stands for Guardians United Against Real Dangers. If there's a **real danger,** the wolves will **protect** our mobs. And players are especially crafty, so we can only take the best."

I grinned at her, and she smiled back nervously. Weirdly, the other two High Commanders looked even less confident. They must have been worried about the other pups in my recruit class. After all, I was

High Commander Wendy Wolf's son.
I was **destined** to be a top GUARD.

"As you know, our GUARDs undertake
dangerous assignments to survey,
secure and protect all the mobs in
Minecraft from our enemies," Okami
barked. "They need specialized skills
in combat, stealth and intelligence.
Today is combat training," Okami said.

Everyone began stretching and
warming up. I'm sure I wasn't
the only one imagining myself as
a **furry ninja,** although nobody
looked as cool as Okami did with his
samurai sword strapped to his back.

"First, we practise a wolf's most basic and most lethal move: our **BITE**."

Oh, I was already **SO GOOD** at biting! I had bitten loads of things in the past — steak, cheeseburgers, my tongue ...

We got partnered up. I was a bit disappointed when I got stuck with Lobo again, because I wanted to work with Felicia Fang. I kept watching her warm up while Okami explained the exercise.

"Do you even know what you're doing?" Lobo asked.

I scoffed. Just because he had come first in every single lesson so far, it didn't mean he was better than me. **I'd show him!**

"Of course I do. We have to bite each other."

Lobo frowned. "What? No, that's not what the instructions — "

"AND BEGIN!" Okami yelled, so I **jumped** on Lobo and quickly bit him on the ear.

He **howled** and tried to fling me off, but I got hold of his scruff and shook. It was a great move because now I was behind his head and he couldn't reach me.

I could probably get a takedown from here, but I wanted to earn **extra points** by showing off my skills. I released Lobo's scruff and pounced on his tail. **BUT I MISSED!** He ran away, yelling something about sticks at me.

SCAREDY WOLF! There was no escaping me! I chased after Lobo. **This was so much fun!** I was really starting to get the hang of this training stuff. I was going to be a great GUARD.

Some of the other recruits stood in my way, so I bowled them over. **I was closing in on Lobo!** He tried hiding behind a pile of sticks, still yelling something at me, but I wasn't listening. I **bashed** right through the pile and the sticks flew everywhere. I **leaped** onto Lobo and we both rolled backwards.

I'D CAUGHT HIM! I landed on top and as long as I stayed there, I would be the winner. In the struggle, his leg pushed in front of my face, and I knew what my last move would be.

CHOMP!

"AARRGHHH!!!"

I fell off the dogpile, grabbing my aching foot. **I'D BITTEN MY OWN LEG!** How did I not notice it was my own foot?!

"WINSTON!"

Everyone was running over. My mum checked my swollen foot.

"Did I win?" I asked her. When I looked around, nobody else seemed excited.

"Um ... Didn't you listen to Okami's instructions?" Mum said. "You were supposed to practise **biting sticks** in half, **not attack your partner.**"

OH ... That explained why Lobo kept running away and yelling about sticks.

"Oops," I said sheepishly. **"SORRY, LOBO!"**

Lobo just glared. His ear looked kind of wonky where I'd bitten him.

"You also knocked over your entire team," Okami said. "You didn't listen to the instructions and you were not being a **team player.** I'm afraid you would not make a good GUARD. You should go home and think if this is really the right job for you."

I didn't know what to say. Was I **FAILING TRAINING?!**

I looked at my mum. She was one of the best GUARDs the Den has ever seen. She tried to smile, but I could tell she was **disappointed.**

I left the training grounds, limping on my bitten foot. **ALL WOLVES** grew up to be GUARDs! **What would I be if I didn't too?**

It was hard to fall asleep last night with all the **worries** in my head. Whenever I thought about my mistakes at training, I felt so **embarrassed.** Did Okami and the other recruits think I was a bad wolf? Did my mum? I was too nervous to ask her so I'd gone to bed without dinner.

When I woke up this morning, our

cave was empty. Mum had already left for work, but there was a tasty breakfast left out on the table for me. I smiled. **Mums are the best.**

Okay, if I didn't become a GUARD, what else could I be?

A shepherd? Nah, I'd probably chase the sheep away.

Cartographer? Hmm ... I'm not great with directions.

Professional gamer? Cool in theory, but wolves don't have **thumbs.** Makes gaming tricky.

By the time I finished breakfast, I still didn't have any better job ideas.

Training was on again today – maybe I just needed to try harder. Maybe training was just going to be more challenging for me than it was for other pups. If it took me a bit more time to learn, that wouldn't be so bad. Besides, I know that Mum only wants me to try my best.

So I would do my best.

But once I got to GUARD training, everything was much busier than usual. The recruits were standing off to the side while official GUARDs ran around doing **important jobs.** The High Commanders were busy barking orders into their earpieces. I was nearly run over by Intelligence GUARDs and Tech Support DOGs bringing in maps and secret files.

"What's going on?" I asked the team of recruits.

'There's been reports of disturbances near the Den,' Felicia told me. "Players, probably. If they discover the secret entrance —"

"Our whole operation would be **compromised**," I realized. This was a serious security threat. **Players** liked exploring and wrecking things, and the HOWL Council were always worried they'd find our secret base.

"It sounds like our Stealth Squad and Strike Force GUARDs are all off on other assignments in the Overworld," Lobo said. His ear was still a bit swollen. "There are **no teams** nearby to deal with whatever trouble these villains are cooking up."

Wow, no wonder Mum looked worried right now. She growled more orders through her earpiece and then came over to us.

"It could just be a **false alarm**," she tried to reassure us. "Our warning scanners keep beeping, but our best teams are too far away to check the perimeter. The High Commanders could go and look, but then there'd be no-one left in the Den to lead and protect our home."

NO-ONE TO PROTECT OUR HOME?!

An amazing idea occurred to me.
"That's not true!" I said. "YOU HAVE US!"

"Winston, what do you mean?"

High Commander Okami and High Commander Rolfe walked over to listen.

"We might only be recruits, but we want to help protect our home," I said. Felicia, Lobo and the others nodded. **"YOU COULD SEND US!"**

"As a training exercise?" Mum looked doubtful. "I don't know..."

"It could be **dangerous**," Okami warned.

"We could really use the intel," Rolfe said. "What if they just went outside the Den, checked the area and reported back? Then we would know how serious the threat is."

The High Commanders talked quietly for a minute. I looked around at the other recruits. I could tell they were excited. **A real assignment!**

"Okay," Okami said finally. "Recruits, you are **CLEARED FOR DUTY.**"

This was going to be the best day ever! The GUARD recruits and I were going on a real assignment!

We were all shown some maps of the local area, but I got bored and wandered off. I peeked through a door and found an engineering lab where a lone wolf with welding goggles was working on what looked to be an invention.

"Hi! Are you an inventor? **THAT'S SO COOL!**"

"**Thanks!**" the engineer said with a smile. "But the HOWL Council says GUARDs don't need snazzy inventions to do their jobs, so no-one ever really uses my inventions."

"What sort of things do you invent?" I asked her. Her name badge said "Edwina".

"Combat and stealth tech, mostly," she sighed. "Gadgets, that sort of thing. Stuff nobody in the Den has any use for."

I looked around the lab at all the cool stuff she had built. I **couldn't believe** the HOWL Council weren't putting it all to good use! I nudged a bodysuit lying on a lab bench.

"What's this for?"

"Oh, it's just a high-tech multi-suit with a range of special sensors, teleportation capabilities and built-in armour," Edwina said with a **shrug.** "Nothing too fancy."

NOTHING TOO FANCY?!

"**Wow!**" I exclaimed. "Can I try it on?"

"Really? SURE!"

Edwina helped me put it on.
It was a perfect fit! But when
I looked in the mirror, I couldn't
see **anything!**

"No-one will be able to tell you're
wearing it because it blends into our
fur pixels," Edwina said proudly.

I was **AMAZED!** She excitedly
showed me the buttons hidden
where my nose could press them.

I picked up the last piece, which
looked like a high-tech collar.

"That is my latest invention!" she said. "It's an Anti-ADORBS collar — Anti-Antagonist Deflect-O-Ray Beam System. It's meant to fend off enemies, but it didn't work in any of the field tests, so now it's **junk**."

I put it on. It was perfectly **CAMOUFLAGED!** There was a button on the shoulder.

"Why didn't it work?"

"I don't know! I tested it against skeletons, zombies, even ghasts. It just never did anything except shoot **love hearts** out everywhere. **SO EMBARRASSING!**"

"Maybe it only works against certain enemies?" I suggested.

"Winston? Where has he gone?" Outside the lab, someone was calling for me. Oh yeah, my assignment!

"Thanks for your help, Edwina! Mind if I borrow these?"

"Go ahead," she said. "No-one else

wants my inventions, after all."

Their loss. I ran out to wait with the others. In my rush, I accidentally stood on Felicia Fang's paw and bumped some other pup into Lobo. He was in the middle of sharpening his claws with his teeth, a delicate task at the best of times, and when he got knocked, his teeth chipped the razor-sharp claw edge. So we had a bit of a delayed start because Lobo needed to file his claw, and then we were off!

"Please be careful, Winston," Mum said when we reached the secret exit to the Den. "I know you want to prove yourself, but don't do anything dangerous."

"I'll be **fine,** Mum," I said. "We're only gathering information to report back. I'll stay hidden and focused and – **ARE THOSE EARPIECES?!**"

Oh man, it has been my **DREAM**

for so long to get my own earpiece.
Proper security gear.

"Yes," said Okami, as he handed
each of us an earpiece. "These
are only a temporary loan for this
assignment so you can report your
every move."

"**CHHH,** putting earpiece into
earhole," I whispered. "**CHHH,**
turning head. Walking one block.
CHHH, scratching ear. Earpiece
fell out —"

"Not your **every** move, Winston,"
High Commander Rolfe sighed.

"Or if you need help," Mum added. "This is a training exercise and you are not cleared for combat. Which means that if you *are* faced with an enemy, you must retreat somewhere safe and contact us. You are **NOT** to attack. Do you all understand?"

"Yes, High Commander Wolf," all the recruits said.

Mum looked doubtful, but Okami pushed the button to open the Den's secret entrance. Heavy-duty metal doors slid apart to reveal thick trees, and we all blinked in the morning light.

The High Commanders wished us luck and I gave my mum a **wink.** I would be fine. This whole thing was **my idea,** remember? What could possibly **GO WRONG?**

The recruits and I sneaked out the doors of our secret underground compound and moved past the trees that hid the entrance. We heard the quiet hum of the doors sealing up tight behind us. Now we were on our own.

Kind of.

"Winston, can you hear me?"

"Yes, Mum, I can hear you. These earpieces are **SO COOL!**"

"We will try not to talk to you too much so you don't get distracted," she said. "Remember, you're only looking. GUARDs deal with real dangers — it's in the name — and there are **more than** just players out there."

No enemy would get the better of me! I was going to stay well clear of them. I knew there were a lot of dangerous things in the Overworld, like creepers, zombies and skeletons ... any one of them could create trouble. And once I saw **trouble,** I'd be sure to let my mum know so the professionals could take care of it.

We sneaked around for quite a while without seeing anything suspicious. A few times I tried **leading** the team, but then Lobo or Felicia would overtake me, and it all got a bit confusing because we didn't know who was in charge. So I asked them.

"Hey guys, who do you think is **in charge?**"

No-one replied.

"Guys?"

They looked at me, but no-one said anything. Maybe their ears were blocked by their earpieces. I turned my earpiece microphone up.

"Do you want to take it in turns being in charge, or — ?"

"SHHHHH!"

Oh, yeah, the silence thing.

"Sorry!" I whispered loudly so they could still hear me. "I said, do you want — "

Lobo seemed to lose patience.

"Listen, Winston," he whispered, coming close to me. "Don't you think that tree stump looks really suspicious?"

I looked around and spotted a tree that had been punched over.

"I guess?"

"A player might have messed with it," Lobo whispered.

I frowned. Players often interfere with biomes. They **dig up** minerals, knock **down** trees and try to **construct** things. I'm not sure why.

"You should stay here in case the player comes back," Lobo suggested. "We will look further ahead, then regroup with you."

It sounded like a good idea, so I agreed. I nestled into a bush to hide while the other recruits **tip-toed away.**

"Anything to report?" Mum asked in my ear.

I shook my head, then remembered she couldn't see me.

"Not yet. I'm **staking out** some possible player activity," I whispered. "Can't talk, concentrating."

I stared hard at the stump and waited. And waited. And waited...

My team didn't come back.

After a while, I started to get worried. I'd been sitting for **HOURS** and my team hadn't come back. At least, it *felt* like hours.

To make matters worse, my tree stump hadn't moved. Not that I expected it to. I just wanted something exciting to happen. But not a single leaf blew and not a sound reached my pointy ears.

Why hadn't the other recruits come back? Had they run into **trouble,** or gotten lost? Maybe they'd gotten into some **CRAZY COOL ACTION** and lost track of time, or maybe they were hiding like I was.

"Hey, guys?" I whispered into my earpiece microphone. "Is everything alright?"

Silence.

"Uh, I think you might have forgotten to come back for me?"

Still no reply.

So weird. I mean, it couldn't be that they left me behind **on purpose,** right? I switched channels to communicate with the Den.

"Mum? I mean, High Commander Wolf?"

"Winston? Are you okay?"

"Yeah, Mum, I'm fine. Just wondering if you've heard from the other recruits?"

"No, not for a while," she replied over the radio. "Why? Have you run into any players or other enemies?

Do you need backup?"

"No," I sighed. "No player activity
here. And I don't need backup.
I can do stuff on my own."

"There's nothing wrong with needing
help," Mum said. "That's why GUARDs
work together in teams, so they can
help each other solve problems."

I said goodbye and tried not to
feel **annoyed.** Even my own mum
thought I wasn't good enough to
handle problems **BY MYSELF!**
Maybe Lobo did leave me behind on
purpose. Maybe he thought I was

holding the team back because of all my mistakes. That made me feel **sad.**

I was still alone with my tree stump. I should head back to the Den, I wasn't helping anyone out here. I stood and stretched all my tired muscles and stepped out of the bushes.

Then the CRAZIEST thing happened!

Right in front of me, a **PLAYER** appeared out of nowhere. Like, he just spawned there. And he was

STARING RIGHT AT ME!

I guess I panicked. **A PLAYER?!** For a second, I wasn't sure what to do. The High Commanders had said not to get into combat with any enemies, but what if it **attacked me?** And if I ran away, what other trouble might a player cause?

Then I realized what an **amazing opportunity** this was! Strike Force GUARDs who defeated players were always the most admired. I was finally going to prove my combat skills. Everyone would be so **IMPRESSED**. My mum would be **so proud**.

I growled and hunkered down into predator mode. This **foolish player** had messed with the wrong wolf! Winston Wolf, future Guardian United Against Real Dangers, was about to eat him whole!

I stabbed my **sharp claws** into

the dirt and prepared my **powerful** back legs for a magnificent leap. The player looked nervous. He stuck his hand behind his back. Good, all the easier to tackle him down. I let out a **SCARY GROWL** to really terrify him and got ready to

POUNCE!

But at that exact moment, the player threw something at me. A **BONE** landed on the ground, and I stopped growling.

Um, what? Who just casually throws tasty bones around? I was so **confused.** Not to mention **hungry!** My tummy grumbled.

I looked at the player. He wasn't moving and didn't seem dangerous. And, listen, I know you're not meant to take food from strangers, but I had been sitting behind that bush **ALL DAY** and I needed the energy to fight him. So I quickly gobbled the entire bone.

SO YUM! I swallowed and licked my lips. Where did he get such a good bone from? I was about to ask him, but then I realised I wasn't sure if players were smart enough to talk. I'd never met one before.

Maybe if I pounced at him now, I could check his pockets and eat any other bones he had ... I licked my lips again.

But then he threw another bone to me. **I couldn't believe it!** I snatched it up and crunched it between my teeth. **DELICIOUS!**

He kept throwing bones at me and I kept eating them. But now I had a problem. If I attacked the player, he wouldn't be able to get me any more bones. I was chewing on my fifth tasty bone when the most **brilliant** idea struck me.

I knew exactly what to do.

I needed to tame this player.

"OM-NOM-NOM-NOM."

I let the player throw me a few more bones before I put my genius plan into action. You can't scheme on an empty stomach, after all. Plus they were **so good!**

THEN IT SUDDENLY SPOKE!

The player, not the bone.

"This has to be a glitch," the player muttered as he threw me yet another bone. **"Taming** isn't meant to take this long."

He was right. This taming process was taking a long time, and I was getting full. I sat down on my back legs while I thought about how best to make this player **my pet.**

Biting or growling at him would not make him tame, but maybe something in my high-tech body suit would help? Sensors, teleportation, armour ... Hmm, not very useful for taming.

Then I remembered the camouflaged collar Edwina had given me. I turned my head and pressed the **secret button** on the side. My Anti-ADORBS collar turned red. **COOL!** Even if her technology didn't really work, it still looked neat.

But then big red hearts lit up around me. Edwina was right — that was **embarrassing.**

I guess the player got confused and thought I loved him, because he got really excited and started yelling about the taming process.

'IT WORKED!'

Oh wow! **I'D SUCCEEDED?!** I'd never heard of a wolf taming a player before — maybe I was the **first one ever!** Mum was going to be so proud of me, and the other recruits would be so **amazed.** I couldn't wait to show off my new pet.

The player took a few steps away, and I **followed** after him. He laughed and ran so far and so fast that I lost sight of him. Luckily the sensors on my suit helped me keep track so I activated the teleporter to take me directly to him. I didn't want him to get lost and scared, after all. He was so **helpless.**

Then he told me to sit, which was kind of him because I was pretty tired. I whined in relief as I sat down.

"THIS IS THE BEST!" he said, and threw me some cooked meat.

YUM! Having my very own pet player was going to be awesome.

"I'm going to name you **Brian,**" I said fondly.

"YOU CAN TALK?!" he asked, nearly falling over in surprise.

"Um, of course! Wolves are the smartest and most organised mobs in the Overworld."

"That wasn't in the tutorial," Brian said. Then he smiled at me. "Well, a talking wolf is even better than a normal one! What's your name?"

"WINSTON WOLF. It's a pleasure to meet you," I said with a little bow, grinning proudly.

Brian looked confused, which was only natural since players are not very bright.

"Uh, okay. It's nice to meet you too, Winston! My name is — "

"Brian," I said pleasantly. "I know."

"No, I mean my actual name is — "

"Brian," I said again. "I know because I just named you."

"But I already have a name," he insisted, "and it's — "

"Yes, yes, that's very nice, Brian," I said loudly. Turns out players are not very good at listening! Maybe you need to talk more slowly so they understand. "DO. YOU. HAVE. ANY. MORE. OF. THAT. COOKED. MEAT?"

Brian sighed and got some out of his pocket. I wagged my tail in excitement. Taming a player was definitely worth the effort!

"What's your favourite colour?"
I asked.

"Green," Brian replied.

"What's your favourite song?"

"Don't have one."

"Alright, what's your favourite ice cream flavour?"

"Rainbow."

"Wait, what does a **rainbow** taste like?" I asked curiously. I'd been trying to get to know my new pet and I was learning all sorts of **fascinating things!** "Does it taste like the sky?"

"Nah, it's just food colouring. It tastes like caramel." Brian looked at me suspiciously as we walked together. "Are all tamed wolves this ... chatty?"

"Caramel, interesting ... Personally, I can't decide between llama with choc chips and rab — hang on, what's this about *tamed wolves?*"

I'd never heard of such a thing! Wolfkind are **wild, MAJESTIC** and **INTELLIGENT.** How could anyone tame us?

"Yeah, tamed wolves," Brian said. "Players can feed bones to wolves to make them loyal and they'll wear collars and follow their masters around. Like you."

I NEARLY FELL OVER!

"ME?! A TAMED WOLF?" I burst

out laughing. Brian was so deluded.

"**Of course!** See, you're wearing a collar now, like a pet," Brian said.

"**This?** Oh, you're **SO FUNNY!** This isn't a *pet* collar. It's my Anti-ADORBS collar." I could hardly talk through my own laughter.

"Your **what?**"

"It's **very advanced technology,**" I explained. "You probably wouldn't understand. Anyway, I'm not wearing this because I'm a pet. It's part of my gear. I activated it."

Brian clearly didn't get it, so he changed the subject.

"But you *are* following me around like a pet dog," he pointed out. I just chuckled and shook my head.

"I'm not following you — I'm walking *next to* you to hold a conversation.

That doesn't make me tame."

Brian threw his hands in the air like
I was driving him crazy.

"You've literally followed me
everywhere since we met!"
he said.

"I didn't want you to get lost!"

"I threw you bones and it made
you tame!"

"No, I **let you** throw me bones and
I enjoyed them," I said. "I tamed
you so you would feed me more."

"Okay, Winston," Brian said. "I'm sick of arguing with — wait. **You think you tamed me?!**" Brian looked shocked and ... amused?

"YES!" I yelled, frustrated.

"Um, wow, okay. Well, I spy with my little eye a wolf that's a bit **delusional.** That's not how this game works. I'm the player. You're the wolf."

Game? What game? I didn't know what he was talking about, but my genius wolf brain focused in on another word he'd said.

"Did you just call me a **spy?**" I asked curiously.

"What? No, I — "

But I stopped listening. All of a sudden, everything that had happened over the last few days **made total sense** — my mistakes at training, Okami's comments about my other talents, the questions in my head about other jobs.

I *wasn't* meant to be a GUARD.

I was meant to be a **spy**.
A SECRET AGENT.

Secret agents solve crimes in different ways to Minecraft GUARDs. Rather than protecting mobs against troublesome enemies, a secret agent would investigate strange occurrences and examine crime scenes to work out what happened. The HOWL Council didn't have any secret agents yet. I would be the **only one.**

I HAD FOUND MY DESTINY!

And I'd even found the one thing every secret agent needs — **a partner!**

I'd never been so **sure** of anything in my life. I had found my calling. I was a **SECRET AGENT**.

Or I would be, once I solved my first case.

"I don't think I have time for crime-solving right now," Brian said when I told him what we needed to do. "I just heard my mum say dinner will be ready in ten minutes."

"Oh, does your mum talk into your earpiece, too?"

"What? No, she yelled from the kitchen that I have to hop off my game soon."

I still didn't know what game he was talking about, but it was a good reminder. I should make contact with Mum and the other High Commanders at the Den to tell them my news. I had **TAMED A PLAYER!** They weren't so dangerous or troublesome after all.

And I was going to start a new career as a **secret agent!**

I was about to talk into my earpiece, but at that moment I heard the unmistakable sound of wolves howling.

"THAT'S A DISTRESS CALL!"

I gasped. "My squad needs help!"

"Now that makes more sense!" Brian mumbled to himself. "I did think it was odd that you were alone. Are the other three nearby?"

"Why do you assume there's three

of them?" I asked, eyeing him suspiciously. "Doesn't matter. Are you going to help or not?"

The wolves were still sounding the **distress call.** Brian listened for a second.

"I think they're nearby," he said. "I might have time if we hurry."

I was keen to hurry! My squad of fellow recruits could be in **serious danger.**

"You said these other wolves are your squad?" Brian said as we ran in the direction of the howling. "Is that what you call it when wolves spawn in groups of four?"

"They're the other GUARDs-in-training," I said. "We were all learning to be GUARDs together, but when we got reports of enemy activity near our secret base, we were chosen for a field exercise. Wait, you're not an **enemy spy,** are you?"

My suspicions returned. I hadn't considered this possibility.

"Nope. I don't even know who the enemy is," Brian said.

Hmm, good point.

Even though Brian was a player, he seemed pretty harmless. So maybe players *weren't* the enemy.

But if players weren't responsible for the trouble afoot in the Overworld, then **who was?**

Suddenly, I knew.

"Baby turtles, obviously."

"WHAT?!" Brian started laughing. "For real? Wolves are at war with baby turtles?"

"Not yet, but they will be once I expose baby turtles for the **villains** they truly are," I said darkly. It all made sense now. I thought back to the boring assignment reports. How had no wolf ever realized this before? "My team and I were out looking for troublemakers, but we got separated."

I told him about the tree stump and how Lobo suggested I wait for player activity. Brian grinned.

"Yeah, I did punch that tree over earlier today, but it sounds like your team left you behind on purpose."

Obviously Brian was wrong. Nobody would ever abandon me. I'm too **adorable**.

"I mean, you're pretty annoying," Brian went on. "And you never stop talking. It would be hard to be **stealthy** with you on the team."

"And it's hard to be a secret agent when my junior partner keeps **MISSING CLUES!**" I reminded him. I sniffed the ground and pointed to what he'd almost stepped on. **"Look!** Wolf tracks and tiny footprints. My team came this way, but so did — "

"Baby turtles," Brian said, surprised.

We followed the prints carefully, me snuffling along.

Suddenly, I found an **earpiece**.

"Oh no."
I stuck
my nose
in the
air and
sniffed as deep as I could …
There it was. The unmistakeable
STENCH OF EVIL. "My team has
been led into a trap!"

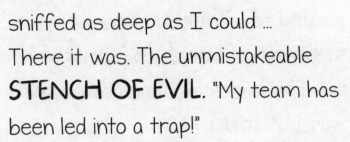

And they wouldn't be able to radio for help because their earpieces had fallen out during the fight. Nobody would **suspect** the baby turtles. I sneaked up to some rocks to look over into a clearing below.

"How did you figure that out from some footprints and a bit of tech?" Brian asked. I shushed him and he came closer.

"First of all, those prints and that earpiece are **clues**," I whispered, "and second, I know they are trapped because I can see them!"

Brian scrambled up beside me so we could both look down into the clearing. **A big hole** had been dug into the ground and inside the hole was my squad! Lobo, Felicia and that other recruit whose name I could never remember were **trapped,** surrounded by —

"BABY TURTLES!" Brian whispered. "You were right!"

I nodded. A whole **GANG** of baby turtles stood around the edge of the hole. It was so deep that my classmates couldn't jump out. The turtles must have **tricked** the wolves into falling in.

"What do we do?" Brian asked.

My tummy did **flips of fear.** Who knew what despicable plans the baby turtles had devised for the recruits? I could radio in and report the situation to the Den, but my mum and the other High Commanders would never get here in time to save them.

It was all up to me. I had to do something now or I might never see them again.

"We have to **rescue** them," I whispered. "Are you any good at fighting?"

"Well, I do have this," said Brian, who then casually pulled **A SWORD** out of **NOWHERE**.

"That'll help," I said. "Are you ready?"

"I can't believe I'm saying this," he muttered as he stood up. Then he yelled, **"WE'RE COMING FOR**

YOU, BABY TURTLES!"

We jumped over the rocks and ran at the enemy. They barely had a chance to turn around before I caught one in my jaws as a warning.

"Give up, **villainous fiends!**" I shouted, but it burst into a puff of smoke.

Probably teleporting back to headquarters – **COWARD!**

"You don't know who you're messing with!" the **lead turtle** squeaked.

Then, out of their tiny little shells they drew **tridents** and pointed them straight at us. "Now you're gonna get it."

They ran at us and tried to spike us with their tridents.

"**WHOA!**" said Brian. "This is new! I didn't think turtles came with tridents!"

"**They normally don't!**" I yelled, but we were now in battle. I turned to fend off the next baby turtle and saw Brian slashing them up with his sword. For a pet player, he had some **great moves!**

SWING, HACK, SLASH!

Smoke cloud.

LEAP, SCRATCH, BITE!

Smoke cloud.

I snatched a baby turtle up into my jaws and threw it towards Brian. He whacked it with his sword and it turned to smoke. This was kind of **fun!**

"COMMANDO ROLL!" I cried,

using my best strike moves. "Aim ... **Target acquired!**"

Then I saw Brian pause. A baby turtle was looking at him with its sad, tiny, adorable green face. Brian was being **hypnotized** by its cuteness! No wonder baby turtles never get caught for their crimes. **THEY'RE SUPERVILLAINS!**

"Look away, Brian!" I yelled. But he stayed still, trapped in its sweet sad stare. **"DESTROY IT!"**

"But it's so cute ..." he said slowly, like a zombie. He was a goner.

But not me! I soon realized that Edwina's Anti-ADORBS collar really *did* work. It was deflecting their hypnosis powers, so no cuteness was going to stop me! I finished off the baby turtle in front of me then leaped towards the one trying to brainwash Brian. **THE NERVE!** I'd already tamed this player.

I clamped down on the baby turtle, but its shell was too strong. I spat it back on the ground and it looked at me with its **evil, lovable eyes.**

"You may have won this battle," it said, "but we will be back!"

Just then, a mighty sword came down on the turtle's back, and it immediately disappeared into a puff of white smoke.

Brian had snapped out of the trance and was back to normal.

"WE DID IT!" I realized. All the baby turtles were gone. I smiled at Brian. "Nice job. You know, you make a pretty good junior partner after all."

"Thanks. You were right, the sword did help." He smiled at me, too. "And you are a pretty good wolf secret agent."

"Thanks, Brian!" I felt very **proud.**

"My mum says I have to stop playing now." He put his sword away. "Night, Winston."

And do you remember how he first just **showed up out of nowhere?** Well, now he totally **VANISHED!**

Over by the hole, I heard scratching sounds and the voices of the other wolves.

"Huh? How'd we get down here? What ... What happened?"

It sounded like they were waking up from a hypnotic trance as well.

"HEY, GUYS, I'M COMING!"
I exclaimed.

I found a rope and threw it down to them. They were **amazed** to see me.

"It's Winston," said Lobo. "I can't believe it. You rescued us **ON YOUR OWN?!**"

I looked around for Brian, but he'd disappeared. None of the wolves had even seen him.

"Oh," I said sheepishly, "I guess I did."

Back at the Den, everyone wanted to hear what had happened, but Mum made me file an **official action report** and then sent me straight home to rest. Sleeping felt **so good** after my very long day, and this morning, Mum had breakfast ready for me. She looked like a general with all her badges of honour.

"Reporting for breakfast, High

Commander Wolf!" I said as
I tucked in.

"Winston, we read your report
overnight and everyone is still
confused about what happened
yesterday," she told me. "Lobo
and the others said they were
ambushed in a **surprise attack**
but can't remember who attacked
them or how they ended up in the
pit. They thought they were done
for until you showed up and helped
them climb out." Mum shook her
head before continuing. "We have so
many questions. In your report, you
said you did battle with...

"Baby turtles," I confirmed.

"Right, baby turtles ... Winston, are you sure it wasn't players? They are **tricky** and are always setting traps."

Despite all the proof in the old assignment reports, despite my own description of what happened, **nobody believed me!** Of course, it didn't help that all the baby turtles had disappeared. They'd even removed their tiny footprints, leaving no evidence they'd ever been there.

"It was definitely baby turtles. They are supervillains, Mum. In fact, all

GUARDs should start wearing the Anti-ADORBS collars Edwina invented."

"The defective invention that emits hearts?"

"IT DEFLECTS CUTENESS HYPNOSIS!" I explained loudly.

"Hmm." I could tell she wasn't convinced, so I would need proof. "Well, whatever you defeated, I'm **amazed** you did it on your own."

I chewed thoughtfully. I still hadn't told anyone about Brian, and after Mum's comments about players,

I had a feeling the HOWL Council would be suspicious of any player. Even a tamed player like Brian. They might tell me I couldn't keep him.

"You're not angry I disobeyed orders and got into a battle?"

"I understand you had to act," Mum said. "You're becoming a real wolf, Winston. **I'm proud of you.**"

I smiled and felt warmth in my heart.

"THANKS, MUM."

"Okami and Rolfe want to give you another chance at GUARD training. They think they underestimated you." She paused. "I'm sorry if I underestimated you, too."

She looked sad, and that made me feel sad as well.

"You didn't do anything wrong, Mum," I promised. "Truthfully, I'm not that good at GUARD training because I'm not the same as other wolves. I'm not meant to be a Guardian United Against Real

Dangers. I've found another career path that will be **perfect** for me."

"Really? What's that?"

I puffed out my chest proudly.

"SECRET AGENT WINSTON WOLF, at your service," I announced. "Here to investigate strange occurrences and solve cases for the HOWL Council."

And to prove my theory that baby turtles are the source of all trouble in the Overworld, not players! But Mum didn't need to know that.

"A secret agent?" Mum was very surprised. "I've never heard of a **secret agent wolf**. But if that's what you want to do ..."

"It is. Baby turtles will always be out there causing trouble, and I can really help this way."

"You were definitely helpful yesterday," Mum agreed. "But I don't like the idea of you being alone in the Overworld every day while you work on cases. You know wolves always travel in teams."

"Secret agents don't work in teams,

Mum. **THEY HAVE PARTNERS!** Someone to help spot clues, watch their back, protect them and do jobs for them ..."

"Sounds like they'll get bossed around like a **PET!**' Mum said, and I nearly spat out my breakfast in laughter. "What's so funny?' She said. "And where are you going to find such a partner?'

"Oh, don't worry," I said with a smile. 'I think I know **just the guy**..."

JOIN WINSTON AND BRIAN IN THEIR NEXT TOP-SECRET MINECRAFT MISSION:

UNDERWATER HEIST

BOOK 2 APRIL 2024!

「TOP SECRET」

 Why are we writing it down if it's **TOP SECRET?**

For the future, when I'm famous! Obviously.

 But isn't it risky to write down Overworld secrets? What if it gets into the wrong hands? Or if a publisher makes lots of copies and thousands of people read it ...?

Oh, Brian, your brain pixels must be so small! That'll **never** happen.

WAIT A MINUTE...